G000136741

The story of Adam and Eve is simply retold and delightfully illustrated for young readers.

Note to parents and teachers

There are two accounts of Creation in the opening chapters of the Bible. The story in this book is based on texts known as the 'J' source and can be found in Genesis, chapter 2, verses 4-24. The story of Adam and Eve's fall from grace and banishment from Eden is based on Genesis, chapter 3, verses 1-24.

British Library Cataloguing in Publication Data

Hately, David
When God made Adam and Eve.—(Bible stories)
I. Title II. Breeze, Lynn III. Series
222'.110922 BS580.A4

ISBN 0-7214-0985-7

First edition

Published by Ladybird Books Ltd Loughborough Leicestershire UK
Ladybird Books Inc Lewiston Maine 04240 USA

Printed in England

When God made
Adam and Eve

written by David Hately
illustrated by Lynn Breeze

Ladybird Books

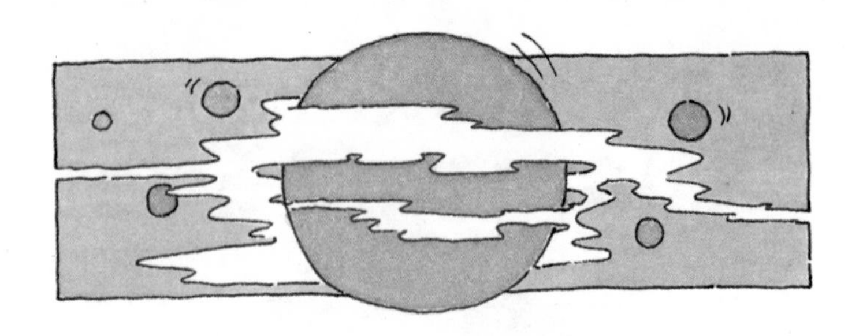

When God first made the world it was like a desert. Nothing grew on it. There weren't any birds or animals. There were no men and women, or children playing.

God saw how empty it all was. So he took some clay from the earth and modelled the shape of a man.

Then he breathed into its nostrils, and the shape started to breathe. The man was alive because he had God's own breath in him.

God wondered where the man could live. He looked at the world, but there was nowhere good enough. So he planted a special garden for the man in a place called Eden.

Every kind of flower and plant and tree grew there, and a great river of sparkling water flowed through it.

In the middle of the garden were two trees. One was the tree of life. God had put it there to show that the man was his perfect friend.

The other was called the tree of the knowledge of good and evil.

The man enjoyed his life in the lovely Garden of Eden. He had to work, for God had put him in charge of the garden. The man liked taking care of all the trees and plants.

God had told the man that everything was just for him! All the fruit, all the flowers and plants, were for the man to enjoy.

But God said that the man must never eat the fruit growing on the tree of the knowledge of good and evil.

'If you eat that,' God said to the man, 'you will learn what it means to die.'

The man soon learned how to look after the garden properly, and God was pleased with his friend. But he thought that the man should have some company. 'It isn't good for him to be alone,' God said to himself.

So God took some more clay, and this time he modelled it into the shapes of every kind of bird and animal and fish. He put them into the garden and gave them all life. He let the man give everything a name.

But God decided that the man needed something more than the wild creatures for company. He needed a partner.

So God made his friend fall into a deep sleep, so that the man wouldn't see the power of God at work. Using some clay and a rib that he took from the man's side, God made a woman and gave her life with his own breath.

The man was grateful for the friend God had given him. The woman

and the man lived together in the garden and they shared everything with each other.

And God, looking at his work, was pleased with what he had done. He knew that the world he had made was perfect.

Most of the creatures living in the garden were quite harmless. But the serpent was dangerous, because it had grown crafty. It was a mischief-maker.

One day the serpent said to the woman, 'Did God really forbid you to eat some of the fruit growing in our garden?'

'We're allowed to take anything we want,' she answered, 'except the fruit from one tree. We have to leave that alone.'

And the serpent saw his chance to make some real mischief.

The serpent asked, 'Which tree do you have to leave alone?'

'One of those growing in the very middle of the garden.' The woman was pleased to tell the serpent all about it. 'Its name is the tree of the knowledge of good and evil. God told my husband that we mustn't eat its fruit.'

'Did he say why?'

'He said that if we eat or even touch it, we will bring something called *death* into the world,' replied the woman.

'That isn't the real reason, you know,' said the sly serpent. 'It's got nothing to do with death, whatever that may be.'

Now the woman was sure that the serpent knew something interesting. She wanted to know what it could be.

So she begged the serpent, 'Tell me the real reason why we mustn't eat the fruit!'

The serpent answered her in a whisper. 'God knows that if you eat fruit from that tree you will become as powerful as he is! He doesn't want that to happen. So he made up this story about death.'

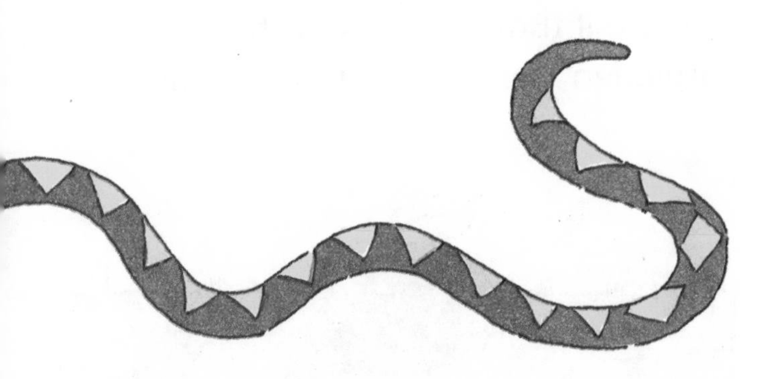

The woman ran off to fetch the man, and together they hurried towards the middle of the garden. She was very excited. She was thinking about what the serpent had said.

She looked up into the great tree of the knowledge of good and evil and saw the fruit hanging from its branches. It looked as though it would be good to eat. She thought about all the power it would give her.

She looked at her husband. She could tell that he wanted the forbidden fruit as much as she did.

The woman stretched up to one of the branches and picked some fruit. Then she bit into it.

Turning to her husband, she said, 'It's good! You try some.'

And the man also ate the fruit that God had forbidden them to touch.

All at once they realised that they weren't going to become as great as God at all! It was their own pride that had made them think that they could be!

They were ashamed of themselves for what they had done.

God enjoyed walking in the garden he had made. His favourite time was in the evening, when it was cool.

But now the man and woman were too frightened to face him. They hid,

hoping God wouldn't see them.

God knew where they were, though. He called out to them, 'Have you been eating the fruit I told you not to touch?'

The man tried to blame the woman. 'I only ate some because of the woman you put with me,' he said. 'She gave it to me!'

The woman tried to blame the serpent. 'I only ate the fruit because of the serpent,' she said. 'The serpent tempted me! It was all the serpent's fault!'

God was angry with the serpent. Its mischief-making had led the man and woman to disobey God's orders.

'You will be sorry for all the trouble

you have caused,' he said to the serpent. 'From now on, because of what you've done, you will have to crawl on your belly and eat dust for the rest of your life.'

Then God turned to the man and woman. He told them that they must leave the garden and never return to it. Their life in the lovely Garden of Eden was finished.

'The land you go to now will be full of brambles and thistles,' God warned them, 'and it will be hard for you to grow enough food even to live on. Just to stay alive you will have to work hard all day and every day. And when your life is over, you will again become the clay I made you from. For what are you but dust? In the end, you will be dust once more.'

As he listened to what God was saying, the man suddenly understood what was meant by death. Their own sin of pride had brought it into the world.

The man and woman went to look for the last time at the two trees standing in the middle of the garden.

The fruit on the tree of the knowledge of good and evil no longer tempted them. It now looked rotten. They wished they had left it alone.

But the tree of life grew tall and green. It still looked beautiful. They cried because they would never see it again.

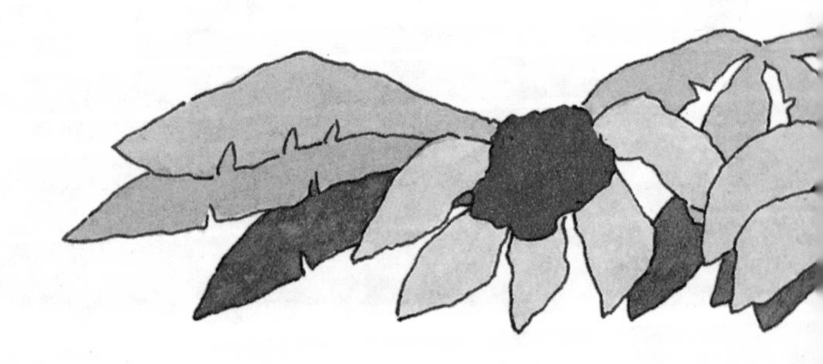

Then the man, who was called Adam, turned to his wife and gave her a special name. He called her Eve, which means *life*.

He gave her this name because she would give life to all the children born into the world. She would be their first mother.

Afterwards, Adam and Eve put on the warm clothes which God had made for them out of animal skins and furs. They left the Garden of Eden for ever and began a new life in the world that God had made.